THE PHONE LOVES THE ADDRESS

A FIGHT BETWEEN LOVE AND LIFE

HIMANSHU RAJ

ISBN 979-888606033-1

This book is dedicated to my dream of being a writer, but that's not enough to write a book many peoples helped me to go through my dreams like my mom dad my teacher's friends, my teammates, and also some YouTubers and writers I am very thank full to all of them.

Contents

Part 1

Preface

This is a story of love and love is the preface of this story .

Foreword

There is no intention to change the world I am very selfish I write this book because I wanted to write it

But in tHIS bOOK tHE PHONE LOVES THE ADDRESS YOU MEET 4 TO FIVE CHARACTERS tHEY ARE GOING TO TAKE YOU FORWARD I THIS STORY WHENEVER YOU NEED TO MOVE ON.

Acknowledgements

I would like to thank my parents who gave me this freedom to write and my friend's teachers and the girl who inspires me always to pick the pen, for her I must say thank you. For whom I have written this book I think that she definitely does not need to read it.

Prologue

I iNVITE YOU TO ENTER IN THIN MY SMALL FICTION WORLD >
AND AFTER THE END PLEASE SHARE WITH ME YOUR FEELING
ON MY G MAIL itsbauua@gmail.com I AM WAITING TO REPLY.

To be what we want to BE

We think that "we just need to do that", But in reality "we have to do that"

(We know little things, but the knowledge, does not affect the reality, the only application can effect so if you think that these small things you know before now, or may you don't know it before till now then this is the time for everyone to pursue his dream and apply the fundamentals)

Then the luck must go on with us or we have to wait till the luck go with us.

We also sometimes need to fight for it, Not only to win, we have to fight because we have decided to fight.

Then maybe sometimes a dream came true

After all that, there is, 'maybe, why?

Some people have the dream put the effort but it does not come true

Sometimes it came true, but for most of the people, "what they get is not his dream",

What they don't get, they focused on that.

"The reality becomes a dream, if we didn't get up"

A great person has said to me that no one can make or break you unleash you are not involved in it.

The toughest thing in life is, I think 'THE DECISIONS'

The story which I am going to present is about someone's decision, Those decisions which created tragedy in his life always. why?

Let's find out ...

HAJIPUR

Hajipur Is a city in Bihar, near Patna. And the best thing about this city is that, "I" love this city, why ?

because my almost all the good and not good memories are from here. So let's enter in this city .

WELCOME

Scene 1

Today , the weather is not good as I am, but the girl in dark grey jeans and in light green top, standing just 8 to 10 meters from me was locking in the sky with a present smile , she is closing her eyes by every degree she turns her head upward , I don't know that just only 8 to 10 meters from me, the weather is so different for her or having a good face and a dog can change everything, ya she is beautiful but not every girl attracted my attention so much before, not only girls, I think nothing has attended my that focus before not even my mirror but till now I don't know that these small differences of just 8 to 10 meter can change the weather. I don't know the girl but there is any connection between us , after all , this happened the very first time in which I was feeling so much she was stranger to me 'but like those who are around her I 'also want to know a little bit more about her .

So I started planning to do something, as "I always" so I put my sharp eyes on the girl for her observation, so I will find anything which can give a start to our conversation.

Her hair is not completely black in color but it was perfect for her .

I think she loves "to play with dog" why, because as much I have seen her, she is playing with her dog whose name is, I think "Pluto" (I am not an astrologer, but I can hear what she is saying to the dog , hey Pluto stop , no Pluto ...)

She now looks at me by making her closer and then she bents a little bit , in quick . I move my head constantly left-right so many times and in between, for a microsecond I also try to look at her, I was shocked when I have seen that the girl started coming towards me, I started calling someone and suddenly my phone drop and from back she says "hey" I turn around and in very confident, I say h, h hi

My legs were not shaking not even my hands, but even after I can feel my nervousness

Before she could say something or I say sorry to her for my behavior. she tries to ask something Mr. Pluto (her dog) picketed my phone and started running, she says that Pluto stop , then I was shocked so I'll look into her eyes and asked what happened , you said something , she replied with a little smile and pointing her hand behind me and said your phone , even now I do not get anything properly till I turn around , I smile a little bit and then we look into each other eyes and we are laughing loudly , As I have told you that the weather is not good like me becasu it was raining and her dog has taken my phone and dropped in a muddy area and my phone is completely destroyed . She said I'm sorry for that,

I think that your phone is gone. I will give you a phone instead of that. after taking some time I said no it's ok I will manage (but in my mind I was thinking that ya please that one was also a very old one) but she was very nice and she gaveded his address and said, on the next Monday you pick your phone, after that she says I have to go in a little warm voice I said ok but wait. She said in surprise, what I said that why you came here, you don't tell and by the way I forget what you said you name. she said till now I haven't said my name I said ok my name is raghav and you she said I am tripti I said ok but why you came here actually I came here because don't get me wrong I think that you are following me oo no no, me and following absolutely not why are you thinking all that she said listen, forget all this we are friends now and put her hand forward we do handshake and she said ok lets met on the next Monday at that address ..... and she slowly turns around and the air blows her hair came on his face she is telling something to Pluto in a little bit loud voice and while telling she gone. I look around to express my the very exciting movement I am feeling like I am wondering and then I leave for my home as mom was waiting for me but wait, what I tell them about my phone, o shit if they know the reality they are going to kill me because this phone is not mine, it's my father's phone, oh no what I'll do, three people are going one of them seems is krish, so I shouted krish, hey krish, he turns around, krish is my friend lives near me so I have trust on him so I tell him the whole story, he said first you'll go and pick up the phone I'll give the water, we return to the incident spot to pickup our phone. in show off I leaved the phone there, krish please do something, ok let's talk to the people around may be they have picketed up, excuse me uncle have you seen a mobile phone here it is in black color cover. he said no my boy, hay brother have you seen a phone here, excuse sister have you seen a phone here after half an hour of search we are unable to find it, now we are sitting on bench, krish is cutting his nails with his teeth in tension and I am making gestures, my legs were shaking and then krish said bro lets go home, you have no idea krish what happens when my father knows how lost his phone. but we are sitting from 3 hours if you do not go home your parents are going to be worried and your number is also switch off , your mom is definitely calling you , Krish convince me to go home , we picked an auto , 40 rupees sir , in surprise I said what , krish said we reached home , I said oh krish put his wallet out then I said I'll give I gaveled the money and we go closer to our door , I make a fist to show me strong but as I'm going closer to bell my fist be becoming loose and loose , ting tong the bell rings , my mom opens the door as she see me , she give me a tit huge and asked where are you from five hours every day you come back between 2 and a half hours , why today you are so much late , are you ok na , hey krish is something happen , I said no mom nothing happens I'm perfectly all right hey krish come in , no I have some work , so I'll have to go and krish leaves . we go inside , mom shuts the door . and then she sit near me , do you want to eat something , no mom I'm fine you'll sit here for some minutes I'll have to say something , mom said ok say it . mom first tell me that , where is dad , mom said he was gone for some of his office work . what happen , nothing mom I hold my mom hands and then on 1 2 3 I said mom I have lost the dads phone . My mom says , nothing to me the sound of our fan is clearly coming I'm making gestures and then I asked my mom hey mom what happened. mom said but how you lost his phone , and wait , why you have taken your dads phone , I said as I am going to walk I saw the phone and that time dad was sleeping I thought , that will come home earlier but ... and the whole thing I said to my mom , mom said in this I'm not going to protect you it's your mistake after all , and how you'll so irresponsible you be , she stands up look into my eyes ,says I don't expect this from you and she goes to her room . I think that this is not so much actually it's just a mobile phone by the way, but I get Goosebumps when think that what happen when dad know, mom is also not in my side I was very worried, then the most horrible sound I heard , ting tong the bell rings. I think it's my dad , what I'll do , I was walking in my hall left right making gestures , and my mom , opens the gate , then she looks at me making her eyes closer , and I think its warning , and yes it is my dad has come , my home has four rooms and a one big hall in which there's two sofa and three chairs in the side of a table , placing at next corner from the main gate so from the second sofa I can exactly who has come and yes it's my dad , I think today I'm gone because its first time when my mom is not between the conversation with my dad , dad ask my mom , what happen today our son Is not in his room by the today he not gone to school , mom looks at me with the same expression and then reply to dad his some test happened previous week so that's why the school has given two days holiday , and in between all this conversation my dad sit next to me and asked how was the test gone , I said good dad , dad says ok mena you got my phone because an important mail is going to come actually its about my first board meeting in which I am going to lead the presentation . I said congrats dad. dad reply oo thank you but go and help your mom to find it , then suddenly mom reply in deep voice yaya ask him he knows better about your phone . Actually dad I'm sorry I am gone park today and there's your phone is missed from me I'm sorry dad,

WHAT, you lost my phone, he increases his tone and again said, but why have taken my phone my dad stands up and said my whole presentation detail is going to come on my mail today look what just happen you in my entire currier I have not the any mistakes and because of this is may the first time and I don't think after that my company is going to give me another chance. Look Nandine Because of your love he is becoming very irresponsible, I tried to spoke up but my mom stops, I know that he has done a mistake but now we have to find any solution for it , you have remember you email password , no I don't do you have any idea son , no mom I said slowly ok you please sit down have some water we will definitely find any solution for your problem then I said , dad we can do one thing we have a forgotten password option so we can try my dad in high pitch ya that's good but again my mom saves me we are on my laptop screen I connected my laptop with the wifi and then open the Gmail then typed my dad it and then I asked him that dad from which no. mail has formed , he said I don't remember completely but may be my 79 , I said ok now an otp has gone on that no. and we are again looking at each other in my dad became more angrier and said but from where I'll give you otp that phone you have loosen na then we again try to calm dad , dad you'll relax we'll do something dad says you do not do anything that better , my mom looks at me and without saying anything she tells me to have patency and after some time my sister Tina came after looking at us she understands that I have done something , she came and my mom tells her the whole situation and the she said dad you can call malhotra uncle na , to send you again that mail on another mail , and after that we all help you in your presentation , after listening all this dad huge Tina and in a relax tone she said oh thanks you solve this very smartly , and then again looks at me she learn something , and with the same expression he said dad forgotten password , useless . I don't mind more because the mistake was mine, now we are at the dining table to have our lunch, I picketed a plate for me then, dad said hey useless you have lost my phone then you have done any complaints for it, I'll at my dad with little bit of regret and said no dad but I'll do that, but the number which is in that phone I have closed it. And with a little conversation I finished my lunch and done the complaint. I was at my bed trying to sleep after all the bad memories of the day, I think I have forgotten the good morning because of that all this happened , now as I remember that girl Neha I remind myself to see the address that where she lives because I have to go there in just three days . So I'll open my purse to see her address but, I was shocked because her address was missing. MY THIS EXPRESSION IS UN EXPRESSIBLE , I was in a shock suddenly I get up from my bed started looking left right , I tried to find it everywhere on the bed on my hall in my drawers everywhere , but while find I was just hoping that any how just I got that but , while finding I know that I was loosen it , and again I gone into my room I was sitting on my bed just trying to remember that where I have loosen it but I was unable to find that , but suddenly I get with a small magical smile I picked a paper and started to write something it was her address because while gave her card , she had told me that that lives near bumping street road no. .. then suddenly with a little stress I was trying to focus , I was telling myself that come on you can do it and I don't remember it completely but I think that It was between 10 to 18 road no. , and then I go to sleep with a lots of regret I switch of the lights and cover myself with a black color blanket. I woke up at 8 PM and at time I was not completely awaken, But her address don't let me to sleep,

The girl Tripti

Tripti talking to his friend neha

Tripti ; hey I am in a deep problem .

Neha : what happened ?

Tripti : actually today I was gone to park with Pluto but there's an incident happened .

Neha : what ?

Tripti : there's I meet someone who is looking so cute , so I want to talk to him but I don't know how ,

Neha : Then you talk to him or not .

Tripti : I have , but there's a problem happened , this stupid Pluto ... and she explains the whole story .

Neha ; (with a loud voice) have you gone mad , you know your parents Na , even after you did this . , you are total stupid , I don't know how you can do this .

Tripti : I know my parents very well that's why I haven't give him my address .

Neha : (suddenly she reacts) then whose address you have give ?

Tripti : yours .

Neha : (don't talk for a minute but) you know very want happened to me in the matter of rahul previous week . Tripti you have not done well to me .

Tripti : (with a requesting voice) hey I don't think at that time but I'll tell your parents everything you just have trust on me . (with sound increasing) and don't forget that in your rahul matter who have helped .

Neha : (calm down) I have trust on you , but have you thought that from where you are going to arrange the money .

Tripti : for that I have called you .

Neha : ok but I can only arrange 3 to 5 thousand . ss

Tripti : o thanks neha but this is not enough almost we need some 20000 rupees .

Neha : ya , in fours na we have to collect the money , by the way you have thought what you'll do if the money I not arranged .

Tripti : I don't know , ok by I have to go .

Neha : ok bye

Now here miss tripti haven't arranged the whole money but ?

And there Mr. Raghav has lost the address what happened next , I don't know . You can think or read next J

Chapter 2 - ….

Raghav loves his mom and dad but his mom was a little bit worrid about his future ,

because he was a little bit irresponsible and his dad thinks he is use less .

Raghav came in depression very easily and again he was in . why because he lost the address of the girl tripti .

Now as raghav have the clue that her home was in between 10 to 18 gully then he decides to go and knock ever bodies house as delivery boy , he thinks that there may me 150 to 200 houses and he have just four days so he called mani his best friend .

Manni : hey raghav why you have called me .

Raghav : I have to find some one house and then he explain his whole story .

Manni : ok bro , let me think something how this will happen .

Raghav : bro you don't take stress I have all thing shouted out .

Manni : how ?

Raghav : As a delivery boy we go to every bodies house and I have just four days , so do it faster .

Manni : but theres one problem bro if we go to every on house with just finding a name then the girl should be in big problem , because any how some people may , can guess .

Raghav : in woried > o shit , I haven't think about it .

Manni

: he puts his hand on his sholder and says bro don't fall in love its our time to rise we .

Raghav : in shock > suddenly what happen to you bro . Are you ok na , what are you telling this rubish .

Manni : with making gestures , bro I'm telling it late but it doesen't means its rubish you have to understand it if you are not I'm today with you and tommorrow wll be with you . your fellings are not wrong but it also doesn't means that they are always not be .

Raghav : I know man , are you helping me or not , I am worid from tommorow and you are saying all this , if you are not solving my problems please don't rise them .

Manni : ok , ok lets think . but remember my words im telling this because I don't want to she you again in that way

Raghav : in a off sound he said , not again repeat all that ,

Manni : shouts , I know what to do

Raghav : also get excited to konow , he ask what ?

Manni : lets call ajay , ajay gupta he is an expet bro in all these matter and if he is going to help I don't thing that something wrong can happen with you .

Raghav : get surprised who his he .

Manni : I know that you don't remember him . you forget always . he is the love guru of our collage and coincidently my good friend also .

Raghav ; how I don't know him . if he was so famous then .

Manni : in a mysterious sound , it's strange , that you don't know him .

Raghav : and why is it so .

Manni : because he plays the guitar …

While he completes his words

Raghav : stops him , you know na , what happened between us how can he is going to help me . and I also don't want to take help from him .

Manni : bro he have forget all that , he ready to be again your best friend ?

Raghav : look in his eyes and in a serious voice said , But I have not and I don't think I will be ?

Manni : exploring his own thoughts > if I more force raghav then the situation my gets critical , let him take his time and after all so many time , he again want live so we need to support him , but what if again suffer with the same pain , no no this time I don't let him such thing like that ,

Then raghav intrupts him and say hey don't waste my time I am already in problem and you are just standing like a statue .

Manni: again starts thinking, why he is not reacting let's forget and follow him, and say ok tell me what I have to do.

Raghav: he hits manni in a friendly and says everything you want that I will explain to you. I called you to help me now just think of it.

Manni: while rubbing where he has hitted he says ok you don't worry everything will be all wright .

NOW THE GIRL

TRIPTI : (thinking) I don't think I am able to collect money . what I'll do what happen he reacheses neha home and found that I have no phone , our friendship is going to end before start . I think I should ask neha that she had thought anything about that .

The phone rings

Neha : HELLO

Tripti : hi , Neha , I call you beacaue I want to ask that you have thinked anything about that blady phone .

Neha : No I have not figured out anything but ya I had talked to one of my friends and she is also ready to give 13 hundred rupees , I know it still not enough but I am really trying my best and listen we have still 2 days right ,so you don't worry we till plan anything

Tripti : well I know you are trying very hard , and thyank you for this supprt . I love you you are my best friend .

Neha : (in a fuuny way she says) I know you very well so even if you don't do the buttring , I'll helped you .

Tripti : haha (trying to laugh) very funny .

Neha : ya mom I am coming , hey tripti my mom is calling , so I call you later .

And the call cuts and then she put the phone down and then she got and a brillent idea for the phone she was very happy , so she call neha but she did not pick up . so she came out from his room with a very big smile . and then her mother hey what hapeend , tripti is just going to kick the table

Tripti's mom : son , be careful .

Tripti : hey mom don't worry , I am very ok . well what you have cooked today .

Tripti's mom : as usual you it's the lunch time you know .

Tripti : but mom I want to eat something right now .

Trpti's mom : I don't have energy to cook righ t now so go and make your self what you want to eat.

THEN tripti's phone rings .

NOW HERE RAGHAV

Manni : bro why do we not go in every gully and talk to there children , maybe we got any friends there.

Raghav : ya we should need to move on after all we can't find every answer just by thinking so this time we need to put our idea , then we should see the result not decide .

Manni : lets go then

Raghav I think I should need to learn riding

Manni before putting his helmet ,says , ya but not now , sit fast .

Hey stop stop raghav says manni what happened we should start from this one

Raghav : hello bro do you know any girl name neha here .

The boy . no bhaiya

Raghav : do you know

Another boy : no bhaiya .

Manni : bro we have searched three galli but we didn't have finded any clue

Raghav : repeats , clue . hmmmm……. hey wait I think I have a one

Her dog

Manni : a dog , which type of clue is this ?

Raghave : not dog pluto , I mean haw many people are are in this city name there pet pluto it's a uniqe one so may be many people knows about that dog(mr. pluto)

Manni : ya you are wright , now I think you should loving dogs bro . but its already 5 PM hapeend so lets now.

Raghav : in a deep voice , if I quit today then how should I call it love . But just to call this love I can't stay there till late night but more half an hour just .

Manni : ok but tomorrow I need somosa then .

Raghav : first you find her than anything you want .

Manni : anything J

Raghav : excuse me uncle do you know ant dog whose name is pluto .

Uncle : no , I live here from 4 years but I haven't heared such name of a dog.

Raghav : ok thyank you uncle

WE ARE NOW READY TO GO OUR TIMES UP , SO LETS GO AND FINISH OUR WORKS AND THEN TOMORROW AT 2 O CLOCK WE WILL MEET AT RATAN SHOP , SIT I'LL LEAVE YOU .

RAGHaV : in low pich , ok lets go , but don't be lake tomorrow .

After reaching home

Raghav : let me take out my shoes , so no body will know anything
.

Raghav's mom : stop there .

Raghav : mom how you'll know , this time I haven't made any
sound .

Raghav's mom : ya I know but I , you forget every time that I'm
your mom stupid .

Raghav : ya very funny . but mom how to do guess .

Raghav's mom : it my time to ask , where are gone today , you
know your dad was very angry on you .

Raghav : tell me something new mom , you know this is normal for
me . I'll explain you everything but first I want to eat something ,
Im very hungry right now .

Raghva's mom : ok but I get something for you . uou go and wash
your hands .

Raghav : I don't know how to explain this to you , I know that you
are not going to belive me .

Raghav's mom ; let me decide everything you just tell me where
are you today .

Raghav : mom today I was gone in a school to give interview for a
teacher , but they also said the same think which I'm hearing from
the past two years .

Raghav's mom : why you do not try anything else , son somethime we need put our dreams aside to move on , so don't let your dreams to be the breaker which stops you from discovering yourself always be open minded , I know that one day you'll be a very good teacher , you know the story of krishn kartika .

Raghav : lean towadrs to his mom and says no mom , but who is he ?

Raghav's mom : He is a student in our collage , and one year seniour to me. In our collage everybody knowss him as a krishn . He was very famous for his story telling , his stories are amazing , once you have heared any story from him then I think you also became a fan of him . Then one day we meet in our canteen , I said hi , your stories are very amazing you can be very good story teller , then he said he want to became an author and he has startd writing when he was in 7th standard , but till now he was just able to write 3 novels but none of them get published . I said that there are many publishing houses . why not you try in any of then , krishn : I have been got rejected from 70 publishing houses , but I have still belive on me I know that I can became writter , but just just being a good story teller , I don't think is enough . I want then to ask more about his writing but his has finished his lunch so he said by to me . and after that we have no conversation between us . He was not a very good in studies so he don't get placement in the campus selection . He belongs from a middle poor family . I thought then that he may get depreasd or do something else then his dreams , but nor his forget his dream nor his just stick to it . He started his carrier as a story teller and from the money he get takes classes about writing. AND now he was a very popular author , his two books has one on the the first and the second one is in fifth place of best selling list .

Raghav : so mom what do you think what I'll do I have noting such extra ordinary talent . means I'm not going to became a teacher .

Raghav's mom : first you should learn to understand the correct meaning , what I want to say is that you'll need to practice more just thinking to became a teacher is not enough , you'll need to work on yourself and YOU NEED TO FIGURE OUT THAT BEING A TEACHER IS WHAT ? UNDERSTAND .

Raghav : give me some time mom to think on that its very deep . so I'll go in my room I have some pending work also . oh mom na on such a small thing she gavded so long speech but what she said to me was 100% correct but she don't know the reality I think should also need to focus on my mom's word she have cares for me so I know I don't need to think about manni problems .

Raghav have seen her mom was hearing his words so then he started to say something else now his mom had gone to his room . He also started to think about the next day on how he will find the address

Now the girl Tripti

Tripti's phone rings

Tripti : I think its neha call . (she was right)

Neha : hi tripti you called me one hours ago .

Tripti : yes I have , because I think I have find the solution for the phone , you remember how my phone was buyed .

Neha : what do you want to say .

Tripti : I just want to say that we can buy a phone on emi .

Neha : ya it's a brilent idea . we can do this but wait today is the sity is closed my dad told me . so we go tomorrow at 10 o'clock .

Tripti : thyanks neha , then you want to anywhere else today , or leave tomorrow we will go

Now the boy raghav the last day

Raghav : hey manni where are you you know I'm waiting for from half an hour . '

Manni : o sorry yaar but when I was coming today I made an accident ,

Raghav : you have not harm yourself na . are you ok ?

Manni : I'm very ok but .But I don't think that the girl Is in very good condition .

Raghav : you have taken that girl to the hospital or not ?

Manni : ya I have done that , but her one leg get frakchered . ok let's focus on work .

Raghav : ok lets go find the address .

Manni : only 5 gali more left this is our last hope .

Raghav : cross his figure and closes her eyes , and says w can't loose this time we have beat our track record of loosing so all the best .

In the left side of the gali there is one tree and then a field and then some houses are there on the right side there is one old house and with some gap then theres a kirana shop and two sutters after that theres are some houses so manni go to the left side and I go the right one

We tried a lot , 4 hours happened , we have asked almost from every one , we can .

Raghav : I don't think that she lives here , I think my guess was wrong , sorry manni for wasting for your time , now just three hours remaind . let me sit on the bench .

Manni : don't worry my friend everything will be all right .

Raghav sits on a bench near the a shop , I offer him some water , Raghav is from childhood was a little bit emotional one day when we are in 5th class we have a friend name devika , we have a very good bond with her raghav have a little stronger , but that year her school get changed she was no more remain our friend , raghav was very hopeless and that feeling is again visible on his face today .

Half an hour later raghav get up and said lets go , I asked him if he was ok or not but he don't answer anything to me , it was expected but ,the thing which I'm not expecting is Raghav silence from the childhood he don't know to hide emotions , he expresses everything everytime . what happened to him in just a meeting I don't know , when he tell me about that girl I don't thing that he was so seriours , and who can belive that in such a very small meeting such strong feeling can form .

Manni : where we are going raghav .

Raghav maintain his silence. Raghav had said to move but he is
not moving from here .

I can't do anything other then wait , raghav is sitting on my bike
and I am standing near the tree

Then after some time an uncle how is crossing to called raghav , he
didn't listen so I'll go near him , hey uncle what happened ,

Uncle : this boy is asking about some dog Pluto , tomorrow

Manni : ya uncle do you know anything about him .

Uncle : ya I have talked to my son about this name so she told me
that her friend have a pet whose name is Pluto , who lives in the
gali no. 23 I think but why you are searching for a dog I don't .

Manni : (with a pleasant smile) uncle thank you very much I'll
explain you everything .

hey raghav lets go the I got the address you don't worry , sit sit
come on

the bell rings hello aunty is neha is there

Aunty : no son , she today have an accident she was in hospital .

Raghav : o sorry aunty , can you tell me the name of the hospital
we are her friends .

Aunty : ok , she is in Hr hospitals .

Raghav : thanks aunty , hey manni lets go to the the hospital .

At the Hospital

Manni : (this is the same hospital in which I have admitted that girl)

Raghav : hello ma'am neha

Receptionist : sorry sir there are two neha which one dare you finding .

Raghav : ma'am I don't know her tittle you tell me the I will check the both one .

Reciptionist : sir what is your relation with the patient .

Raghav : we are her friends , acctually her leg is gone fractured , now could ou help me

Reciptionist : ya sure . 2nd floor ward no. 16 .

Raghav : hey manni what are you doing there caome here lets go .

Raghav is running towards that room

Raghav : Hey she is not neha .

Manni : are you sure because the morning accident I am talking about she is that one . she also that time told her name neha

Tripti was gone to buy some medicine and raghav knows tripti as neha .

Now neha is looking at but don't understand anything then she saw manni , she get a little bit fired she turn her face red makes her eyes brauder looks like she is not going to leave him , after seeing all this manni have not a bit off courage to face her so he decide to stay there but raghav no no bro its all your done so you will need to gone first .

Manni : hey sorry neha I have said in the morning to and even now I am also saying .

Neha : oho thyanks for doing that , you know take your sorry at yourself I am going to take revange for it , you will just wait na . (she takes a deep breath .)

Raghav : (intrupts) are you neha , you have the dog named pluto .

Neha : (the original one) now who is he ? what do you want .

Raghav : acctualy I am finding someone . but you are not she . but I am just confused because how that the dog name can be so similar .

Neha : listen I am neha , my dog also name is pluto but I don't know anything more . a long pause from neha

We are in shock we just can't understand that what is happing its like after a very big strome there's a complete silence .

Neha : (changes her tone in excitement) are you raghav ?

Now we don't understand that what she understand

Hey raghav let me explain you everything myself first tripti and she is neha the address which I have to give you is her and that puppy which you saw that day is also her , I know that you have lots of questions in mind like why have hided my name and the address in the reality who am I

'As I said I am tripti i can't answer the rest of the questions now and I am sorry because I have not arranged the phone yet .

Raghav said : hey don't worry about my , that phone is get repaired so you don't worry for that actually I am here today just to meet you , I don't know that why are you not answering the question but I belive that when you are able to do so you will do , then raghav tries to change the mood of everyone so he called me and introduced me we all became friends now . now its time when the neha's family members came to take her home . tripti introduced us as friend , hello uncle hello aunty myself raghav but they was worried for their child so they don't focus more on us they were looking very worried they take neha to the home , tripti was also moving with them I think that before going she would give her address phone no. or anything which can be the medium of our conversation but she forgets I think that she was not interested in it that ok lets move on I came home today I gave the same excuse the teacher interview I don't talk to anyone I'll enter in my room then I focus on my mom's word . also I want to forget those which I have done these days , this week is not good for me now I was in a deep thought on different topics I also don't know clearly that what I am thinking , just I want to be busy .

The next morning (A new journey)

I was near the calendar today , looking at the today's date it is 13th august 2017. Just before 46 days from now , almost at the same time I was near the same calendar but from that day to today there's a lot of things has changed

I had decided to a lot of things but non of them has completed there still 14 days remain but I don't want to even start . I think i need to learn the game of ludo . I remember , when I was small , I play ludo with my ajay uncle , when we were at the end of the game and I was loosing then he use to tell me that Raghav when you are loosing the game with three players try to loose with 2 in the same game means don't loose with more gap always try to decrease the gap between you and the win . So today I need to go through the same advice and also to through some dice on the board . Its time to play the game . My mom was right I need to change my route for this time , I need some another plain , so that why I thought a lot last night , and i came on a conclusion that I need to open a coaching center now . I can't wait any more for a job . Lets talk to my mom first about this I know that she will support me .

Hey mom , I want to start a coaching center what you think should I move on

Mom . with a proud smile yes son you should move on .

Mom Says I have not thought more about it I think I will make a proper plain of it . by the way what is in the breakfast , I am a little bit hungry .

Raghav's mom say's : come today is your favorite dish I have cooked .

My smile get multiplied after listing this mom .

Ok mom now I have to go , the food was very tasty today , may be I will be late , bye mom .

I have called manni to came at sharp 11 o clock its now 11:30 . oh manni where are you are .

Manni says : bro traffic in this country , manni get off from his bike and say's by the way what happen of your tripti .

Raghav looks in the manni eyes and says look now I am not interested in the conversation of her , give me some time I will get back on it . I have more important topic do you want to talk .

Manni with a polite voice : bro you are like mirror you always bring opposite meaning to my words .

Raghav : hey stop your non sense conversation , I want to talk about something serious . and you are joking .

Manni : no no do you thing it's a joke , no bro . Someone very grate has said this .

Raghav : o really who ?

Manni : ME

Raghav : wait I will tell you . (raghav hits him in a friendly way)

Manni : ok ok I am serious now you say now .

Raghav : look I want to open a cochin center here . So I will need to buy benches and other things also . I have a place also from where we can start .

Manni : you have everything ready . so why are you waiting then .

Raghav : ya I have just plain ready on the paper but I was unable to apply it .

Manni : (in a harsh pitch he says) Why are you unable to apply it is it impossible , is someone is not letting you to do it , tell mw clearly what do you think the problem is ?

Raghav : thinks a lot but he remains silent .

Then manni came put his hand on the raghav shoulder and in in convencing voice he says , raghav I know you from the childhood , you always run away from the problems .

Raghav : what do you want to say , say it clearly .

Manni : listen to me carefully I always want good for you , and I also belive that you can be a very good teacher also . But my friend , This Is the not the right time first you have to clear out every thing between you and tripti , I know that you want to run away from her so that's why you are making yourself busy in your coaching , but think once that , how you will you tech when you are not clear .

Raghav : (In frustration) Listen manni , I don't want to talk all this now . I came here with another reason , So , please do not bring all this .

Manni : raghav please try to understand , ok you just wait for one week then if you do not understand then I will definetly help you but now I can she clearly that you are hiding you emotions , so don't let them kill you from inside , let them came out , make yourself free . And one last thing bro , that y our feelings are not wrong . So don't blame yourself you are right . And I am always with you . I belive strongly from childhood that something special in you , Why are you not accepting that you are treating yourself as a guilty when you are not .

Raghav : hey manni , I do not want to talk you right now . Let me go now .

And raghav goes lives

Manni : raghav listen hey raghav .

But raghav do not listen anything .

I don't know what manni understands himself , he is thinking I am running from problems manni says to himself . What everybody thinks about me , my dad , my friends and relatives also thinks that I am not able to do something in my life , so this time I am going to prove everyone that "I am not a failure" .

THE GIRL TRIPTI

Tripti sitting in his room , Her one hand is on his face and another one is making a stand for her poster . she is constantly looking at a picture which is hanging on the wall .

Tripti what are you doing , her mom shouts .

Tripti what are you doing , her mom again call her for help in kitchen for making lunch . but she was not listing her mom words . then her mom came to she her that what she is doing . the door was half close so her mom pusses that and then go near tripti and her his hand on her shoulder and says hey tripti what are you thinking I am calling you so loudly but you are not answering me , your are ok na .

Tripti : ya ya I am totally fine mom . Just I am thinking about something , but why are you calling me .

Tripti mom says : I am calling you just because I want a little bit of your help in the kitchen .

Ok mom lets go tripti says to her mom .

We go to the kitchen I cut the vegetables , and I am just looking my mom to making her dish , then suddenly small brother Ankit is shouting didi where are you . I says in the kitchen loudly .

Ankit : hey di I have some work of school which is not happing from me so you'll help me na .

Tripti : ok come on I will help you , come come .

Ankit : di this one is not .

Oh stupid look into this chapter you will find the answer . I say

Ankit : di I have tried but I am not able to solve it .

Ok first you read the question . and tell me what it means first .

Then my mom say tripti your phone is ringing .

Then I tell ankit to use this formula and apply like that . you do this , I am coming .

Its neha miscall , I call her .

Hey tripti what are you doing . neha says .

Tripti : nothing you tell why you have called me .

Neha : I have called you because , am just thinking about raghav . we came from there without saying bye to him .

Tripti : oh its not a problem . I think that they can understand the situation .

Neha : ya they can . By the way what next , have you thought anything .

Tripti : what can I think ? I don't know whats going to happen next . you legs are well ?

Neha : yes its good .

Tripti : ok neha bye then I have some work .

Neha : ok then bye .

Tripti is just worried a little bit everyone can feel it . Neha thinks ,
Tripti also wants to do something In her life and she is very good
sketch artist . but she was not able to find opportunity in this field
,because she have not explore it very well . for her , drawing is her
life but her that life Is only on her drawing table . SHE wanted to
became a fashion designer , but her family does not support her so
she quits her studies after 12th . Now after three years of quitting
12th she wants to do something and this is the spirit I want to see in
tripti . She do not know raghav a little but she feels very connected
to him , I think that's called first sight love . I don't know that how
they are going to meet but for my friend I have to do something , I
think I have raghav's friend manni number , when manni take me
to the hospital he has gaveded me a no. let me call on it ,

The phone rings .

Hello

Now The boy raghav

In the park where I meet tripti first time ,

Raghav : I know that I am running from life but they do not know
that why I am running away from life . Actually they don't know
the reality which I am hiding from everybody even from myself . I
wanted to do something from the childhood but those way I have
taken are noting going towards the aim . I can't tell anyone about

It . Now at this point of life I can't loose my best friend . Manni knows that I am here . We had promised each other that we meet here if anyone get angry . He also knows that I am waiting for him here , but still he is not coming . Ok I have no other option , I have to wait for him , and know that he is going to come today .

And after a long wait of 23 mins he manni came hey raghav neha had .....

The Girl

Hello I am neha here , are you mahindar Singh . neha said .

Hi myself mahindar . who are you . manni says

Neha : Oh stupid you don't remember me , you have injured my leg , yesterday and now you'll forget me .

Manni : hey listen I have not forgotten you . just you call me the first time so I did not get you properly .

Neha : I know that you are an idiot but that big you are , I don't know . By the way I have called you because yesterday we leaved the hospital but not get any chance to say bye .

Manni : oh don't mind about that , we can understand . Hey , how you got my no.

Neha : hello these all thing are my friend want to say to raghav , (in a rude voice) we don't mind . And you forget that you have filed your no. in a from . I am not like all those girls who are in search of boys no. don't take me wrong other wise this time I will break your leg , and both one .

Manni : hey don't talk to me like that , I know that I have mak=de a big mistak e but in that only I am not the responsible the whole you know .

Neha : o helo , what do you want to say that accident happened because of me .

Manni : you are taking my word wrongly . I don't mean that , you know.

Neha : ya ya I know you very well what you mean I know . I want to ask a thing also that , someone not hired you for my accident ?

Manni : Hey are you mad ?

Neha : Hellooo , how day you to call me mad . you don't know me .

Manni : ok ok I am so sorry for that , I am mad you are not , Happy ,

Neha : ya that's sound better . By the why I have called you I forget , my friend tripti have something to say to your friend raghav but I forget what she said . Can you send me raghav no.

Manni : ya sure .

Neha : ok I will call you later bye.

Manni run towards the park where he knows that raghav is waiting for him .

The boy

Hey raghav neha had called me just to say sorry for tomorrow she told me that tripti wants to talk to you something , bro everything is going to solve automatically .

Raghav : Automatically nothing happens , and stop kidding to me you right now I am in a very serious mood .

Manni : I know I know , but I don't think that you know the reality , ok you don't believe on me listen to this , you know that in my phone calls record automatically .

Raghav : ya I know . but you do not play all this , right now just focused on my aim so I you want you can talk on that , and yes till now I have not made any clear statement about that girl . so this I am not go to repeat , that's why listen to me very carefully , " Its true that I love that girl , its also true that my nature is to run away from problems and right now I am in that condition in which I trust on very few people" . But it is also true that I am changing . SO please give me some time , I am trying my best . and about tripti we are not going to discus more , I know that I love her but just because of that I don't have any HAQ to spoil her life . So please raghav don't force me .

Manni : I don't know that why are you doing all this but ya ok I trust on you .

Raghav : And manni promise me that about all this you are not going to tell anyone ok

Manni : ok sir I promise .. Now then we are very free , so we can work on your cochin.

Tell me what I have to do for you .

Raghav says : Hey listen , we have to find a room where we can teach.

Manni : hello , wait what do you mean by we , I am not going to became a teacher , its such a boring job .

Raghav : (suddenly says) No No bro you can't do that , we need teachers actually you have to come .

Manni : Listen bro , I can do anything for you , but please , not this .

Raghav : I can understand , But you don't have any choice . You have to come , we have done so much things together , And I am not showing but do you think , I am not nervous . SO you just take deep breath , I will manage everything .

Manni : Ok I am coming , but I tell you one thing if it doesn't suits me then I will leave .

Raghav : ya ya sure . Now lets go , we have lots of things to arrange . And thank you buddy for everything.

Manni : It's done or something more remains .

Raghav : you come , I will show how much things remained .

Its take four days to us to arrange all the materials for the coaching , we do a lot of hard works , we are not sleeping the whole night these days , but after all these efforts we are happy now , we had arranged the room , the benches. But now almost the whole work is done and if we work in this speed then in two days we are able to open the cochin center . The name of our coaching center is THE ADITYA CLASSES . And I am sorry that I have not tell you about Aditya . Me raghav and aditya are best friends in the childhood . WE always stay together we play , we fight , we laugh , we eat , we read we do all things together . Our friendship is going good . But a very big incident happen with aditya , her mom and dad are coming back from her cousin marriage , and while coming they have an accident , in that accident her father get injured very badly and lost his life , her mother both legs get fractured , and she also lost his vision . Aditya loves very much to his dad and after that accident he became very quite . His hobby is to do painting with his mom , Her mom always appreciate aditya painting she put some of his drawing in the kitchen also . but after that accident aditya never draws anything . In one leg of her mom there's a rod , And after that accident they leaved the state because of some reasons . And after that accident aditya and his mom are gone out of the states . I am sorry . I can't say more about him . And because of Our friends name Raghav said me that he does not want to Advertise , raghav wants to open a coaching center not a business .

THE GIRL

Tripti , at his house roof top , taking small steps in deep thoughts . I don't know that what is she thinking , but ya as much I know her she was thinking about , And that is about her life . In the today's world everyone is just doing that , so it is not difficult to anyone to what he is thinking and thinking about your life is not wrong , But in that thinking we forget to live and that is not fair with life .

Tripti talking to her : what I am doing , I left my studies for sketching but what I am doing right now . I know I love raghav A bit I want to do friendship with him but what I am doing . In that two meeting with raghav i get connected with raghav and today I am taking action about my life my passion is all because of raghav

. But right now I am very clear about me . I have doubts but they no more can effect or I can handle them . I can do sketching , But I have to find this time more opportunities how I don't ? But the believe of you can , I think carry me where I want to be .

Lets go to neha house to she her and to also show her .

Our ladders need to be more smaller is difficult for us to take steps quickly . I think I need to take a walk , Ok lets cover the distance with our feet

Tripti :Hi neha are your leg fine

Neha : Right now its fine but some times I can feel a little bit pain around my ankle .By the way you tell me , how you come .

Tripti : I came just to she you and I have to discuss some things with you .

Neha : ya please you do , tell me what you want to say .

Tripti : I want to discuss something with you , its important for me look at this these are some sketches which I have done almost three years ago and these I have done yesterday , I know that the quality is get down but right now I want better than that quality so I have decided to start sketching again

Neha : really , oh really . are you not kidding me na . I think I am dreaming , pinch me you just pinch . oh it hurt , means I am not dreaming . you do not know tripti that from when me and you mom are expecting that you will restart you life , you know when you quit the drawing from your life , I always scares , that you do not take any wrong step . This news is really awesome let me recover then we will celebrate this movement , But now I won't let it go , Neha shouts loudly hey mom I need water .

Neha's mom (Mrs tiwari) : ok dear I am coming . after some time .
take this her mom said .

Neha : mom I need one more glass .

Mrs Tiwari : ya sure , Let me come .

Neha : hey triti pick up this glass .

Tripti : are you gone mad what are you doing .

Neha : suddenly ya ya you just do what I say . ok now cheers .

Hey slowly take the water just feel the movement . oh god thank
you for giving some mind to this non sense .

Tripti : tries to control his smile to show his anger , hey how day
you called me mad .

Neha : ya how I day you to call you you , you are born mad .

And we both starts smiling . These silly thing I have misdeed in the
previous three years tripti thinks in his mind .

We are enjoing the movement then neha suddenly said hey tripti
tell me how you came on the right track , because we have tried a
lot but nothing worked on you , so suddenly what happened . Tell
me ?

Tripti : (2000 years later) just I came back I also don't know how .

Tripti hides his feeling and the reality about his love because she
never shares his feeling with anyone , why ? Nor I know about it or
nor tripti have any idea about it .

Neha : no problem , you just came back its enough .thank you thank you so much , you came here I want to give you huge . she give a tight huge.

Tripti : hey why are crying do spoil all this otherwise I will also start crying.

And from my eye also some drops came out .

Neha : But you know one thing .

Now the boy

Today our coaching is going to open manni , I can't believe on my raghav says

Manni : You just wait few more ours , and then you are going to belive .

Raghav : ya brother , thank you so much .

Manni you just shut your mouth right now , and don't think that you'll say thank you and I'll be gone , nope after all this is my coaching also , Right .

Raghav : with a pleasant smile says right .

Manni do not waste time the opening is today . So work faster .

Raghav : The same thing also applies on you .

At the time of opening we have somehow arranged 3 students from class 10th . and if I say truly then I have not expected this , I have not thought anything like that , I thought that I may got many students but I think this is called the beginning .

Today we have not done something big we just organized a Puja and every thing happed very beautifully there are so many people . My father was looking not so happy but he was also not get angry . ok tomorrow I have my first class so I want to sleep better but today I don't why I am not feeling sleepy .

In the coaching

WEDNESDAY

Today is my first class so lets pray it all goes so good . The students are yet to come . The time remains 15 min but my excitement is on the peak .

The students enter

All three says : good morning sir .

Raghav : Good morning , come take your sits .

So today is our first class so lets begin with introduction . so what's you name ?

Sir my myself Sunil Kumar .

Sir myself Arun raj .

Sir myself Vicky singh .

Ok grate myself raghav . Now give me your book and tell me how much portion you have completed , so I figure out from where we will start .

Arun raj : sir in math's we have completed 6 chapters . so you can start with 7th one .

Raghav : Ok lets start .

After 1 hours

Ok so tomorrow you will revise what I have taught and come .

Ok sir , the students said . But sunil remained quite . now I and sunil remain in the class .

Raghv : hey what happened sunil , My teaching methods are that boring .

Sunil : looked towards me and said ; Nothing sir , I am fine ok sir bye .

Raghav : Ok bye . I remained silent but my mind is still questioning a lot .

But I don't gaveled importance to that . I looked towards the next and that is the party time , as I had promised to manni ,

so I complete my promise and after that manni leaves me at my house .

now days I have formed a new hobby of writing dairy , actually I have heard so many people write dairy , so I also thought that why not I will also try . I thought that this habit will not be maintained for so long , because nothing had been , but it proves me wrong , And now I don't remember that when I have started it to write , but I don't write daily , I write only on occasions ,

Like , when I want to share some of my biggest secretes or when I have to share my opinion with me or when I get upset or when I wants to talk . But today I guess none of them occasions is . I just want to record the day when I had started teaching , and I have noted down that , now the last thing I want to say is I am missing a lot today tripti I thought that If I make myself busy then i have no time for his memories but not happened as I have thought , now I don't know , what should i do ? This is not the first time when is am in confusion , my whole life is just mess of confusion . Not only confusion I have in my life . I have decision making problem also and this problem is not only mine , I think that every unhappy man and women is suffering from this problem . I have no idea about its solution . I think that some problems are not to be solved , They just came in you life for time taking , Like when some one fall in love he or she take lot of time to solve an unnecessary problem , IS SHE LOVES ME ? IS HE LOVES ME ? When they actually get closer to answer then they are unable to find themselves .

I don't want to repeat , all this again .

So the better thing is that , me and tripti stay away from each other .

THRUSDAY

Mom : Hey raghav , wake up now its 10:30 AM get up quickly .

Raghav : Removes his blanket and said what ? its 10:30 , why you have not waken me up earlier .

Mom : what do you think I have not tried .

Raghav : Oh sorry mom .

Mom : Now you be responsible you are a teacher now it is a very tough job and you have chosen this way so you need be responsible .

Raghav : And wait I am not irresponsible .

Mom : I am just joking .

And I continued my coaching my dairy writing and everything and this is my routine for the next 3 months .

After 3 months

In the coaching

Raghav : Hey sunil , why are you not studying .

You are not doing any home work and where is you all friends

Sunil : sir they left . and sir write now I don't want to study but you believe I will start my study from tomorrow .

Raghav : you know , IF ANYONE IS TELLING , I WILL START STUDY FROM THAT DAY ,THEN THIS IS ONLY DISTRACTION POINT NEITHER YOU ARE SEARCHING FOR SAFE ZONE .

Sunil : You bet sir nothing like that is going to happen .

Raghav : That is best .

But things not change not change ,

The girl

Nandini : mam .

Tripti : yes .

Nandini : neha mam has call'ed you . she says me to remind you to make a call .

Tripti : ok I will ,

Nandini : thank you mama . (nandini is the manager of tripti)

Tripti make the call .

Neha : hello mam , you have forgotten me after becoming a sketch artist .

Tripti : no nothing like that , just the work load Is a little bit so no time remains . you tell me how you remember me

Neha : just I want to talk to you . by the way tell me how was your work going .

Tripti : excellent .

Neha : wow I mean just in three months you have achieved so much on the basics of you hard work .

Tripti : forget all this you tell me what are you doing ?

Neha : Nothing special . I am also trying to find a job and I want to do something in life . But there is nothing possible .

Tripti : interrupts neha and said , you know at once my thoughts wore also like the same and from there I am also not able to see my future where I am today . So first you take this thought our from your mind and life also . And lust start enjoying it nothing more or less than that .

Neha : Ya but every situation is not the same .

Tripti : I know that you are not going to understand this today but may be some day my words effect .

Neha : ok then , lets wait till . By the way in last 3 months you tried to contact raghav . Actually I am sorry .

Tripti : I tried but nothing happened . but sorry for what .

Neha : you know that I have raghav friends no. but because of my small brother I lost it .

Tripti : Don't remind me all that , I am already suffering . Ok by I talk to you latter .

Some drops came out from tripti eyes and the silence goes on . Then his brother came .

The boy raghav

Raghav : once again on his table with his dairy

Today the coaching not gone well , sunil is not doing his home work .

He is a little bit attached with me that's why he alone came daily coaching .

HE don't talk much about study when I teaches him some lesions he almost ignore and when I tell him some stories then he haves a lager focus . He ask me lots of questions on life , and from where I bring such beautiful stories about my confidence everything about me . I don't know that what he wants to do in life and I don't want to guess or know , but ya I care a lot about his future he don't knows that but I have also get connect with him . Now the main question came that 3 months happened and there is no sign of tripti iinmy life rather then my heart . I still have a strong connection with her . because of my character , nobody believes that love exists in my life , I also .

But who cares, I don't . In my life there is very less space for emotions I don't show then , I just write sometimes because paper have more patience , but I think I have more patience then paper . I don't know many things about life . but I know a little bit of its secretes . good night .

The next day in the coaching center .

Sunil : good after noon sir .

Raghav : come sit , you have done you home work .

Sunil : you know sir yesterday Is my birthday . AND ayush has sent me a gift that was my sketch . Do you want to see .

Raghav : (Thinking about his mistake that he has chosen yesterday to correct his mistakes) . after some time he says ya give me .

Tripti : HI you are here right now , your study is done or some problem you have .

Tripti's brother (ayush) says : No sister , just I was studding from many hours , so for refreshments I came here . and thanks sis for making a great gift for my friend .

Tripti : From where you learn this .

Ayush : what to say thank you .

Tripti : No , buttering .

Ayush : shouts hey , now stop . what are you doing right now , o nothing , then lets go to have something .

Tripti : Laughs And says no I am busy right now .

Ayush : Hey sis Please take me , I am very hungry and I want to eat something tasty so take . please .

Tripti : ok lets go , and your coaching .

Ayush : oh that aditya classes . I left .

Tripti : why ?

Ayush : Beacuse the teacher who teaches us is teaching well but sunil don't let him to teach he always In a mood of joke . so that's why I lest . But raghav is really great teacher .

Tripti stops : They are just going to reach the shop where they where going to reach but after listing the name of raghav she stop and goes in a deep thought , then .

Raghav : hey sis the shop is not here it is a little bit steps more .

Tripri : then says ya ya .

Then eat but the whole time tripti was in thought .

Ok ayush you go now study I have some works now .

Ayush : ok by .

Now tripti was thining a lot she started finding raghav .

The next day she got the address now she needs something is a reason to go there . Tripti was thinking about the reason from 3 days and she finally got an idea that is ...

The boy

Sunil is her sister name is tripti .

Sunil : yes but how do you know sir .

Raghav : Have look on the sketch there is a signature named tripti .

After the class ends raghav starts to finding that the thing which he is thinking is true or not .

And after his research he knows that she is her tripti . But as raghav has promised to himself he wipe his eyes and again stops himself . but for three days he was unable to control his feeling so he tries to get her number . But he was unable to find then suddenly some one call's him he don't pick that call , but after so many rings , he pick up the phone and say hello

The girl

Tripti : I think I need to call after all I still have to return his phone and she after very hard efforts she finds his number .

She got the number but still she need courage to make the call .

Tripti : typing the no. on the dial pad and erasing it but by mistake she makes the call but raghav didn't pick ups and she made that mistake again and again and raghav picks up the call .

Now THE GIRL AND THE BOY

Raghav : in high pich says : Hi who is this .

Tripti : gets scared so slowly says : Hi

Raghav : suddenly after hearing the voice her feeling change vice-versa and now in a with very expectation says . IS this is tripti ?

Tripti gets Goosebumps , she remains quite for some time when she gets that just by listening my voice raghav recognized that its me , then with a smile she replies that . yes , But how you recognition that it is me .

Raghav : Yes , I have not recognized your voice , your voice is recognizable . But you tell me , How you have made effort to call me .

Tripti : I thought that I still have to return someone a thing .

Raghav : yes your thinking is write but for wrong thing (for me I mean about her heart and she was thinking about the phone) .

Tripti : I will definitely give you but before that you tell me that in between last 3 to 4 months you have not made any effort to contact me . and i have given my address to you ?

Raghav : yes you have given but that day is the most luckiest and unluckiest day in my life . And that day I loose your address , but you forget that whose address you have given and listen I have not made any effort because I am making efforts for someone else , I mean for myself .

Tripti : So let's meet on the next Monday , and you are making efforts for yourself , yes useless friends don't deserve time . suddenly She says , hay raghav lets meet on Monday where we meet first time.

Raghav : nice idea lets meet ,you don't deserve time, no nothing like that madam , That much time you deserve believe me I don't have that much time .

Tripti : suddenly says , what .

Raghav : nothing . you tell me what are you doing right now .

Tripti : I am a sketch artist . And a art teacher also . And you what
are you doing .

Raghav : I am just a teacher nothing more then that .

Now from both side the questions remains no more and we don't
want to say by so for some time we talk in silence after that .

Raghav : ok so you'll text me your address and lets meet on next
Monday .

Tripti : ok

Oh this life is amazing , everything is just revolves around me and
I am tiring to make distance . raghav thinks .

Now wait for the next Monday (3 days)

3 day's remain

Raghav just anyhow these three days goes . what will have for her
on that day , I am sure she is going to give me a phone I also have
to give something to her . oh what that gift will be the best thing I
can't make any compromise in it . I have to think my level best .
and the whole days goes in thinking that .

2days remain

The last night is very long these night only came In my life before some of my favorite occasions or on some other special days .

Let's go to our coaching to think . But nothing coming in my mind . While going to the coaching center I saw some name plates with very simple but beautiful decoration . And don't know why I was the whole time thinking about it there is a lots of other best things like some cloths shop some gifts corners also but nothing attracts my attention . so I thought that I need to give her something address specific . And the best part is that after thing the idea only I became happy , I don't know that the main problem is going to come because what can someone think to give just address specific , what I am going to say tripti hay I have an address for you or what . I am very stupid . who gives some one a address . hey raghav you wasted another day .

The final day

(The final chapter also)

Raghav (Thinking) that just 2 hours remain in our meeting and I have nothing to give her .

Tripti : is almost ready she is now just waiting for time to happen . she was also thinking that may be raghav is having some gifts for me and after so many time I am going to meet him .

The Time has come

Raghav is waiting for tripti in the park

Tripti is waiting for raghav in the park

And raghav saw her coincidentally this again tripti was 8 to 10 meters from him but now she was more beautiful and this time I know her the girl in Black dress , She Is tripti .

And now I have something for her but she is not here to take it

Actually 10 years happened

We meet 10 years before

In ten years I wrote a book for her named The address

Which she calls , That the phone loves the address .

THE END